I celebrated World Book Day 2021
with this gift from my local bookseller and
Hachette Children's Group

#ShareAStory

Also by Sita Brahmachari

For all courageous dreamers - S.B

ORION CHILDREN'S BOOKS

First published in Great Britain in 2021 by Hodder and Stoughton

1 3 5 7 9 10 8 6 4 2

Text copyright © Sita Brahmachari, 2021
Illustrations copyright © Poonam Mistry, 2021
Extract from *The Forest of Moon and Sword* © Amy Raphael, 2021

A CIP catalogue record for this book
is available from the British Library.

ISBN 978 1 51010 914 8
Export ISBN 978 1 51010 915 5

Printed and bound in Great Britain by Clays Ltd, Elcograf S.p.A.

The paper and board used in this book
are made from wood from responsible sources.

Orion Children's Books
An imprint of
Hachette Children's Group
Part of Hodder and Stoughton
Carmelite House
50 Victoria Embankment
London EC4Y 0DZ

An Hachette UK Company
www.hachette.co.uk

www.hachettechildrens.co.uk

THE RIVER WHALE

SITA BRAHMACHARI

Orion

Can't sleep.

My mind keeps meandering to waving Usha off on the coach this morning. My sister Usha. I wonder how she's getting on without me on her 'outward bounds' trip? Better than me, I bet. Knots tangle my belly with missing her.

I suppose this *is* the first time I've ever tried to sleep on my own up here. Back when I got adopted a year ago, I wondered if I would ever sleep in a room with Usha and now I'm struggling to see how I'll sleep all week without her. Funny how quickly you can get used to a new normal.

I let my eyes rest on the anchor sunken into the middle of the room. Soft light glows through the enormous 'Globe Window' that once belonged to some ancient ocean liner. Hard to believe now that this ship-like room ever gave me the creeps, but then it did to our friend Cosmo too the first time he came up here.

What he whispered in my ear when he set eyes on the anchor gets me thinking ... What *would* it feel like to be Usha – to know your granddad cared enough to design a world like this for you? A dreaming room to let the troubles of the day wash away. I wonder if she's managed to get to sleep in her dorm? Bet that'll come as a shock. Bit of a role reversal: me here and her in a dreary dorm!

I reach into the last fading sun-shaft and watch it turn my skin and a million dust specks golden.

That's what it would feel like to be Usha … golden! *This is your home too now, why can't you feel it?* I close my eyes and listen to the sift and sway of grasses out on the top deck garden…

shhh   shhh   shhh

I was starting to believe that this all belonged to me too, but it's only taken one day since Usha's been away for me to feel like an outsider again. Now I see, without her by my side I'm not anchored here at all but back to being the old random drifter, arrive-with-nothing-Immy.

I wish Usha's Pops Michael – the grand designer of this dreaming deck – could have been my granddad too.

I wish he'd have words for me ... say, 'This is all yours too, my grandchild. Now steer this ship and dive into your dreams.'

The chronometer's ticking fills my head

the clock that doesn't tell the time

but helps to navigate through water

collected from a distant shore

I raise the conch shell to my ear

losing myself in wave after wave

Long grasses bend on the breeze
through the Globe Window

drawing me through

and out to sea

Dive into my dreams

forget the kit

snorkle

oxygen cylinder

mask

Forget forcing my body like sausage meat
into the clinging skin of a wetsuit

zipping in

too tight

fitting feet into fins

Here I am

Immy Joseph

no safety checks

or theory tests left to take

just me swimming solo

dream-diving down

The wave-roar in my ear mutates
to the old chords

lowing deep

the whale song that always
used to help me sleep

Sonar sound plays me

I am the chord carried on waves

towed on currents

hovering in the lido's water column

sinking

till my belly grazes the
diamond path of lanes

and I'm lying on the bottom

The distant call of the chronometer's now

tap tap tapping at the tiles

Breaking time

the pool cracks open

and I'm swimming into

aquamarine

startling

sparkling

Blue Planet

Ocean

light

Almost free

more whale than human

entering a bright clean watery world

rainbow fish dart at my eyes

shoals of fluorescent colour

too shimmery to be real

drifting   floating

swirling

emerging

expelling glittering fountains

breathing in again

before returning

moving slow and sure through wild water

in dreaming distance

let me go

into the wild

let me swim free

But thoughts pincer into me

*Please let me stay in **dream time***

There is nowhere I want to be more

but like it or not I'm blasted back to the
waking-shore

MUST PREPARE FOR DIVING TEST

foghorn thoughts

bolt me upright

If you don't pass tomorrow maybe you never will.

If I get my certificate Clynton's got to keep his promise before he goes off travelling.

'Here's an incentive for you, Immy. Learn your theory. Complete all your technicals tomorrow and I'll take you wild swimming before I leave. No more pool confines.'

But do I know the theory well enough?

Nerves niggle

like

shoals of nipping fish

darting through the theory in my head

Clynton's dive-safely instructions in my ear.

I wish Usha could test me one last time. Maybe driftwood-doubts are rushing in because *everything* feels like it's switching up new again. Bad enough that Clynton's off on his travels soon and Usha away, but why did our form tutor have to go on the trip with her too? School will feel so strange tomorrow, just Cosmo to hang out with.

Did I definitely lock the Globe Window?

Get a grip, Imtiaz. You're not even on your own.

Our kitten Rubey's curled up beside me sleeping peacefully.

Take a dream-dive, Immy.

I pick up the conch shell

from my bedside table

press it against my ear

to lose myself again among the

conch-wave chords

whale chords

I gaze at my whale poster

drifting

beyond the frame then

peer into the viewing lens

to take the 'virtual under-river tour'

from our family outing.

Floating now to the voice of the marine biologist

her commentary

memory

'THEY SAY THE RIVER USED TO BE DEAD.

BUT NOW WE'RE WORKING TO KEEP IT CLEAN,
REGENERATE...'

Imagination sways

to river-bed words

Sea purslane

                    Golden samphire

                                        Salt marsh

        Aster

                    Glasswort

I'm drifting on flower-tides

taking in

the treasure haul

I dream

to swim wild here

to see what can't be seen above the water line.

'HERE THERE ARE EELS

DOLPHINS

SHARKS

SEAHORSES

EVEN SOMETIMES WHALES

THAT LOSE THEIR WAY.'

If only I could see these for myself some day.

Diving in rivers

oceans

seas

Maybe I could do without meeting a shark

Clynton says

Don't worry they won't bother you

with all your bubbles and your kit

but they do.

Heart races as sharks shunt me down

into the darker deep of sleep

Sharks circling my head now

nosing me into a rusted

barnacle encrusted

underwater classroom

seats and desks encased in a heavy metal frame

Icy cold down here

I float in beside Cosmo

a wheel's turning on his desk as he fixes a puncture

I search for our classroom door but

Nothing's where it was before

In place of our tutor

 a tentacled teacher

appears to mess with my brain

I open my mouth

and gag on the grey water

as it points at me and Cosmo

but he's clueless

lost in his repairing

Teacher's eyes are hollows

empty skull cavities

fixed on me

Mouth-slow-motion-mutating

morphing sludge-sound

splurging words

I don't understand

Tentacle arms grow frantic

gesticulating

fingers of floating weeds

entangling

singling us out

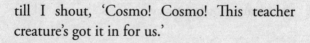

till I shout, 'Cosmo! Cosmo! This teacher creature's got it in for us.'

Now weeds worm into my ears and Cosmo's too

screaming right into my mind

'Please, please, please … turn the volume down?' I beg

Tendril teacher sneers loosening its locks from a tight clasp

not hair at all but

a mass of coiling eels

This close

up in our faces

the bleary words convey

'Today, Immy, I have come to take you and Cosmo into my tendrils.'

I open my mouth but no sound comes out

Wake up, Immy

you've been here before

you know the meaning of this

drift-wood

doubt-dreaming

Get yourself back to the waking shore.

Despite my tears

my wish to rise

the creature's voice is in my mind

clawing at my insides

Cosmo blocks his ears

'Don't let it get to you. Do what I do – find your anchor, sing a song until it's gone.'

'But I can't … can't …'

'What do you dream of being after you've left school? Speak now, Immy!' Tendril teacher orders.

'Don't say!' Cosmo whispers in my ear.

Hair-eels coil into my brain

forcing the words

out

'Mar-ine Bi-olo-gist'.

Scolding laughter in my ear

high-pitched

jeering

sneering

hollow eyes peering

'Immy, dear! Pay attention! Listen to me!'

Tendril-fingers prodding

'Time to face reality.

       Forget   about   your   dreams   of

deep-sea diving

Swimming with whales and dolphins

honestly

Don't you know only the few are

privileged to have a whale's eye view

and in my humble opinion that's not

you.'

I grab ensnaring tendril weeds

thrashing at their clinging hold

pummelling my mind

shrinking my dreams.

The louder its voice booms

the smaller we grow

me and my friend

Cosmo.

'We gotta get out of this nightmare, Immy

look it straight in the eye

try, Immy, try

get up in its face

It can only hold us here if we let ourselves be seen through its eyes

hold on

Kick! Kick away!'

Clinging on to Cosmo's tiny bike wheel together

seats slide from under us.

'And where do you meaningless minnows think you're going?

You have not been dismissed... You'll spend the day in Reflection

if you don't get right back to your seats.'

Gagging on its words

the creature belches plastic bottles

turning water into vomit-murk

growing thick

an oily poison-slick

'Face facts, you two…

There are whales

and then there are barnacles'.

Block ears

block mind

block feeling

Swim towards the red-rimmed orbs of its eye hollows

fill open hearts with underwater flowers …

Sea purslane

Golden samphire

Salt marsh

Aster

Glasswort

Wading through the jellied thickness of its eye

push on through

holding our breath against the slurry stench

jabbing at its lashing voice

until   far

in the distance

we spy

blue

Watery space unfolds

fins still flapping furiously

till we're clear of the creature

free

heart

beat

slows

Inside us sounds the steady beat of the navigation clock

and tick by tock

me and Cosmo begin to grow

Swimming clear of fear

we stare down through Cosmo's spiralling spokes

to

junk-filth

dirt-murk

debris

a colossus of scrap

Pile-up of plastic bottles

the carcass of a rusted car

metal shards

a jagged piece of corrugated roof

a water butt

even

an old iron

floating in the water column

between land and river silt

sinking down

swerving so it doesn't knock us out

I reach for Cosmo's hand

when out of nowhere

we're surrounded

by stellar sparks of light

A herd of seahorses

      sway towards us

switching moves to water music

turning Cosmo's wheel into their dance floor

our eyes are

moon-orbs of wonder

as we come face to face with

the sparkling spirits

of tiny water-dragon guides

I wish they could always be near

but as if in fear

they turn as one and disappear

through the spokes of Cosmo's wheel

at the slow approach of

a

    vast

        black

        underside mottled

        humpback giant of the water

a River Whale

        Gasping for breath

            can't surface

                not yet

              not yet

        no choice

need more

but eyelids open on the waking shore

Why is it when you're desperate to escape from a dream you can't and when you're just about to get to the best bit, you wake up?

My whole body aches. It doesn't feel like I've been dreaming. More like … swimming for days. I yawn wide enough to make my jaw ache. Don't even know how I'm going to get through school today, never mind try for my diving certificate this afternoon. My head's still eel-clogged.

Rubey stretches as she wakes and I pick her up, snuggling into her downy fur, calmed by her purr. I try to shake off the randomness of my dream-dive with … *Cosmo!*

Maybe I can throw a sicky. But how would that work? Make like I'm dying then perk up after school to go diving?

No, I'll have to go in but what I can't get over is how that Tentacle Teacher's tangled with my mind.

What if it was some kind of dream warning that I'm about to get into deep trouble?

What if now that Usha's not in school all week, the drama I had before in Primary, with my reputation going before, comes back to haunt me?

I settle Rubey into a snug cushion and wander past the anchor to the bathroom.

Splashing my face with cold water, I have words with myself in the mirror.

A dream's just a dream.

'Sent to Reflection!'

Sort yourself out, Immy!

I check out the state of me. My hair's all flat so I spike it up again. I must have really been thrashing around last night. I smooth my fingers over my eye shadows and it comes to me in a flash as sudden as dancing seahorses, shining a torch into my brain… I get what my dream meant now. I say it out loud to my face in the mirror as there's no one else to hear.

'Come on, Immy. Time to face your fears.'

After breakfast Cosmo calls round for me. It's too weird seeing him in reality. Like we've faced this monster together, only he doesn't know anything about it. On my way out Mum and Dad make a fuss, give me a bear hug and wish me luck for the test later. As we walk away they're still muttering on about how they would have loved to see me dive.

'Bye, Mum! Bye, Dad!' I call back guiltily, knowing that they could've come to watch me … if I hadn't lied about the no spectator rule.

'So you don't call them Tanvi and Lem any more?' Cosmo asks.

I shake my head. 'Not for ages.'

He looks like he's expecting more of an explanation. To distract myself from the weirdness of dream-Cosmo, as we walk I tell him about when I started to think of Tanvi and Lem as Mum and Dad.

'The night before my birthday I overheard them say they couldn't really afford diving lessons but they would stretch themselves because it was my dream.'

'You and Usha are so lucky. If I wanted to dive I'd have to teach myself,' Cosmo says.

I pause for a minute. 'Do you? Want diving lessons too?'

'No. Not really. Just saying,' he shrugs, 'but carry on...'

'Well, the next day they gave me lessons for my present and I was so excited that "Mum and Dad" just slipped out of me ... and because of what they put in the card:

Dreams are always worth investing in, especially your children's dreams.'

'Sorry.' I yawn wide to hide the emotion gurgling up in me as I finish telling Cosmo.

He gives me a double take. 'You look well rough today.'

'I couldn't sleep. Had this duff dream.

Freaked me out. You were in it.'

He raises his eyes and shoves me in the side as we pass the library. 'Go on then! Don't leave me hanging.'

By the time I reach the bit about Tendril Teacher I seriously wish I hadn't bothered. At the mocking look in his eyes I stop. 'What?'

He can't hold back any more and the laughter blasts out of him. 'I thought Usha was the one with the wild imagination,' he manages to splutter out. I huff-off so he has to run to catch up.

'Immy, I didn't mean to dis your dream. Come down to the barge later and tell Gran about it. You know she's into her dream-reading...'

'I'm so over it!' I lie.

'Look,' he says, managing to keep a straight face now. 'Gran told me once that seahorses have like magic powers. If you were dancing with seahorses I bet it means you'll pass your exam and dive like a whale ... or something!'

We stop at the crossing to school and he grins at me. 'And *I* was dancing with you too, right?'

I scowl, angry at myself for blushing.

'As if!' Cosmo elbows me in the side as we cross the road. 'Come on or we'll be late. Don't want to be thrown into *Reflection*.'

We're hardly through our classroom door when I gulp a huge sigh of relief to see that the supply teacher's nothing like the tendril creature of my nightmare.

He introduces himself as 'Mr Marin'.

Cosmo writes the name down on his rough book and adds an 'e'.

Marine/Sea /creature teacher from your dream? Spooky!

'Shut up, Cosmo,' I mutter.

Mr Marin starts with an association game we play so he can get to know our names. We have to think what we would be if we weren't human. There's a slip of paper on our desks that says:

Name:

Non-human being:

Mr Marin doesn't seem to mind the way we all chat on. I watch Cosmo fill his in, shielding his paper so I can't see. 'Is it your obsession? A golden eagle?' He shakes his head and shows me.

Seagull!

After I've filled in my name my pen hovers…

'No prizes for guessing what you are?'

I *was* going to put *whale* but just to wipe that smirk off his face I write seahorse instead because those dragon-light creatures have lit up my mind.

Mr Marin's made a whole new kind of register.

Dizzy Dingo

Matheus Monkey

Cosmo Seagull

Immy Seahorse

Jayatree Turtle

When we've gone around the whole class and
the laughter's died down Mr Marin asks about
our hobbies. 'Time to test-drive that dream,'
Cosmo jokes, fluttering his fingers like spook-
tendrils. I ignore him.

When it comes to Cosmo's turn he says, 'Fixing
bikes, yeah, cycling mostly. Racing maybe…'

My turn.

'Scuba diving. I've got an exam today,' I say.

Only a tiny bit of me thinks that Mr Marin
will transmutate (is that even a word?) into the

tendril creature and his eyes will turn hollow and spout poison-doubts at me…

But instead he smiles from ear to ear and says, 'Wow! Immy Seahorse! Ever watched the *Blue Planet*?'

'Have I ever breathed?' I say.

On the way out of class Mr Marin wishes me luck and after that I feel all bigged up.

'You sure I'm allowed to watch? If your mum and dad aren't invited I don't see how I am?' Cosmo asks as we head out of school towards the lido.

'To tell the truth, they were actually allowed but I thought it would make me nervous, them being there without Usha. So I made out like they weren't. Anyway, they're busy with work now.' I shrug. 'I don't want to think about it!'

Because now that I've shaken off my dream, I feel light again. In the diving zone.

As we reach the lido door Marsha at reception's chatting on the phone. She holds up her hand for us to wait before we go through to the changing rooms.

'Clynton, man! I've never heard that excuse before, but yeah! She's just arrived. I'll pass you over!'

Raising her thick-lashed eyes to the sky, Marsha hands the phone to me.

'Immy, so sorry to cancel, but I've been called up by the River Divers. Got a bit of a situation here. You wouldn't believe it! There's a young humpback that's lost its way in the Thames and she's in trouble.'

Sonar energy surges through every nerve chord.

'Immy? Are you still there?'

'Serious?! A whale! No way. Where?' I manage to say, gulping down shocks of dream-waves.

'Serious. Yes way! Dartford.'

Clynton always echoes the way I chat. Usually it makes me laugh but right now I'm too weirded out for that.

'Send my apologies to your folks. You can re-schedule the test with your new teacher.'

'But you promised you'd—'

'I know. I'm sorry but I didn't reckon on being called on to save a whale… Hang on, Immy.'

In the background I hear him organising to get a lift on a trauler. Clynton's voice is tight, like he's about to snap when he asks…

'How long will it take? She was last spotted breaching about *an hour ago*.'

He's back with me now. 'I'm really sorry about today, Immy, but you'll do brilliantly with your new teacher. I'll come back to see how you're getting on some time, and maybe one day we'll get that dive in the wild…'

I'm not even going to get to say goodbye.

I feel like I did in my dream last night

why is it always me

being left

missing out?

I'm not giving up without a fight

Charged with sonar power

of dream-diving

and this whale's lost chord

pulses through me

'Now what? 'Cosmo asks as we head out into the street. 'Want to come back to the barge? Tell Gran that your weird dream came true? She'll love that!'

Why is it that everything feels more loaded between me and Cosmo without Usha here, like he's asking me out or something?

'Cosmo! Didn't you hear? In actual real life a whale's in the Thames. I have to get down there. Come too if you want.' I shrug, trying to make it seem like I don't care either way.

'OK!'

'Then let's pick up the tandem. Know the fastest bike route to Dartford?' I ask.

'Yep. Turn left at our mud flat and follow the river.'

We sprint back to my house, hanging on to the railings outside to catch our breath.

'You must have read about the whale somewhere? That's why you dreamed it – they call that "subliminal". Know what that means?'

'I expect you're going to tell me,' I sigh.

Cosmo sticks his tongue out at me. 'Anything "sub" means beneath, below…'

'I know that!'

'But subliminal is below the line of what you think you know…'

'Stop banging on, Cosmo!' I say as I turn my key in the lock, grab Usha's helmet off the hallway hook and pass it to him, ignoring his do-I-have-to-wear-that-thing scowl.

'It's rush hour,' I say. 'You don't want to get knocked uncon—'

'Subconscious! That's the word I was looking for.'

'Just stop going on, will you.' When I've clipped my neck strap closed and waited for Cosmo to do the same we head for the hell-hole of the under-stair cupboard. As we struggle to haul the tandem bicycle out plaster dust falls on our helmets.

'Here's another one … subterranean.' Cosmo laughs off my groaning as we carry the tandem down the steps, get our balance and ride away.

Just when I think he can't have anything left to say, he perks up again!

'And did you know that male seahorses give birth?' Cosmo shouts back at me.

I shove him hard in the back. 'Yes!' I say. 'Now just shut up and pedal.' All I can think of is seeing my river whale.

We're speeding along, way too fast, though I'd never let on that I'm bothered. Even when me and Usha are at full speed we're never this slick, whipping in and out of the traffic like I never knew you could on a tandem. Careering along the cycle lanes, my knuckles turn white from clinging on.

We arrive at our favourite mud flat in half the time it usually takes. Clambering off by Tower Bridge, my heart's thudding hard and my back's coated with sweat. I try not to sound puffed out as we carry the tandem down the steps.

At the bottom Cosmo asks if I'm OK.

'Why wouldn't I be?' I say, dazzled by the sparkling river. Dancing seahorses flash through my mind as we slowly push the tandem along the narrow path of concrete walkway.

'Get your breath back before we carry on,' Cosmo says but my attention's caught by people busying themselves, heading towards a jetty. The way they fly around like bees in a hive all charged up, working together, draws me in as they board … not exactly a boat … more a container raft. There are old tyres stuck to the metal's turquoise, flaking paint. On the side it says in red letters:

'THE BARNACLE.'

'It can't be…' I whisper.

'What?' Cosmo peers at the raft too.

'That's what Tentacle Teacher said in my dream to put me down. "Some people are whales, some are barnacles"…'

'You're having me on! You must have known the Barnacle boat was here all along.'

'I swear I didn't.'

Cosmo laughs. 'Subconscious, subliminal, just saying,' he mumbles.

First the whale, now the barnacle…

'Don't believe me then,' I say, grabbing the tandem as if I'm ready to ride away without him but I'm still in shock as I watch the buzz around *The Barnacle*. Passengers slinging on yellow jackets like they're regulars. As one woman passes I catch sight of a 'River Cleaner Volunteer' label.

Then I spot someone wheeling on an orange trunk just like the one Clynton brings my diving equipment in. Now I tune in I realise I know that deep, echoey voice. Then I spot him standing on board, pointing this way and that, ordering people about.

'That's Clynton. We've got to get on!' I tell Cosmo, pushing the tandem behind a tree to stand with our backs to Clynton, shielding ourselves from sight, listening to him chatting on.

'Looks like I'm the only diver they've managed to get here. She's a juvenile, and by all reports she hasn't surfaced for far too long... I'll go down and investigate. Just a few enthusiastic River Cleaners with me, that's all. If more of the diving team arrive in time, fine, but we can't wait any longer.'

Clynton hangs up, checks his phone, shakes his head and raises his voice. 'Can I make a request – looks like the news is out on social media but if you'd keep your phones switched off, at least for now. We could do without the press on our tail.'

His voice fades away as he disappears into the bright blue tarpaulin-covered area of *The Barnacle*.

'Coming?' I take the handlebars and push the tandem down the ramp. Cosmo's forehead crinkles in a frown but he follows me anyway. We bump the bike across the metal boarding plank seconds before it's raised.

'Feels like home.' Cosmo grins and moves away, over to the far railings, to watch the seagulls dipping and diving on the water, leaving me to deal with the bike.

'Oi!'

I freeze, feeling eyes burning into me.

I suppose it must be the Captain walking down the steps towards me. Strange how he looks like he's in costume, like a vintage sailor in his cap. Why do I feel like I've met him before? Maybe he's been to the lido. My mind's racing, wondering if I should come clean and shout for Clynton so the Captain doesn't throw us off. But right now he seems more interested in the tandem. He places a hand on the front seat and smiles, then nods over to a crate. 'No one boards *The Barnacle* without a life jacket. I'll look after this old treasure. Used to have one myself back in the day!' He winks at me and then over to Cosmo and pushes the tandem away.

Weird! I think and head over to Cosmo, who's leaning on the railings, looking out over the river.

'This feels like a dream, us sailing today,' he says softly, smiling at me as I hand him a jacket.

'Put this on so we blend in,' I whisper.

Pulling up the hoods as the fresh breeze sings in our ears, we sidle over to sit on upturned crates beside the River Cleaners, chatting away so excitedly they don't even notice us. On all their lips I hear the same words about the awesome unexpected reality they never dreamed they were in for today: to get a sighting of this River Whale.

We keep our heads turned to the water, out of Clynton's way, watch the river gliding by,

seagulls track us as Cosmo follows their flight,

knowing what I'm thinking.

Cosmo Seagull!

'I like the way they look so free,' he says as we watch the sea-*birds* cutting through the air, weaving, swerving, gliding…

Like you on your bike, I don't say.

The air smells of salt and steel. A chimney pumps plumes of smoke that leave a tangy-tar taste on my tongue and makes me cough.

How are they allowed to pollute the air like that?

As the river widens it feels like we're heading out to sea… *purslane*

              Golden samphire

                          Salt marsh

     Aster

                             Glasswort

            eel

seahorse

                         dolphin

            river whale

'OK, we're approaching Dartford now.' Clynton's confiding in one of the River Cleaners – an old grey-bearded man. 'I'm going to dive where she was last sighted. As you know, there's a mountain of underwater debris still to clear.'

'You think she's tangled up in it?' the old man asks.

'That's the fear.' Clynton nods, his face all stress-ridged as he checks his phone. 'Well, looks like no other divers are going to make it.' He opens his orange trunk and starts kitting up. I peer in. Like I thought. My stuff's there, ready for my lesson. My heart's thudding so loud with the wild idea that's entered my head that I think Cosmo might hear it.

'Keep your face turned away in case he spots us,' I tell Cosmo.

'What if he does?'

As Clynton prepares himself, the River Cleaners' chatter fades out. I hear someone whisper, 'This shouldn't be a one-man job.' Then silence and the sloshing of waves against *The Barnacle's* bow.

All kitted-up, Clynton climbs down the wide steps on to the platform and lowers himself into the choppy brown water. The River Cleaners lean over the edge wishing him luck, Cosmo among them … so I take my chance, grab my equipment and drag it under the tarpaulin. Huddling under, I strip down to the costume I changed into at school… This has got to be an all-time speed-record for squeezing myself into a wetsuit skin. As I pull on my fins I rehearse the drill, checking off what I have to do.

Cosmo's calling my name now. I will him not to give me away but when the Captain lifts up a corner of the tarpaulin, peering under, I think he has until I see that he's all kitted-up too.

'Coming?' he asks. 'If the kit fits! I believe your wish is to dive and I won't allow you to go down on your own. Captain's rules,' he says, winking at me. 'I haven't dived in years, but there's life in the old sea-dog yet.' He points to some small steps. 'Let us take our leave by a humble exit. No need to draw attention to ourselves.'

There's no time to explain even to myself why I trust this old stranger. But, as we crawl out from under the tarpaulin and head for the steps, quietly lowering ourselves into the water together, I know I do. It's instinct now to check the oxygen dial as Clynton's taught me to.

The Captain salutes and down we go

before I dip below the surface

I raise my arm and wave to Cosmo

as he yells my name

again and again

His voice follows me down

subliminal

                              subconscious

        subliminal

Eyes blink hard

catching sight of the rusted hull of a boat

ear balance sways

Brain builds with familiar pressure

that I used to hate

before I understood that

this is the porthole I must pass through

to bring me back to my sonar self

I am nothing but
                 energy and light

                         as

                                I

                                        sub

                        merge

beyond the border of sound

Swimming through time

guided by beat after beat

of the chronometer clock

feels like I'm dreaming but I know I'm not

I circle

searching for the Captain

A hand presses my shoulder

Clynton's

wild gesturing

signing

questioning

How? Where did you come from?

I sign an 'O' for OK with my forefinger and thumb

and try to find a way to silent-say

that

'I am fine

I dived with the Captain

I'm here to help

we can all dive together

Clynton, the old captain and me'

he shakes his head

disapprovingly

but takes my arm as we swim on

I keep peering behind

Where has the Captain gone?

but Clynton won't wait

keeps pulling me on

No whale in sight yet

then we feel it

the river bed stirs a flurry of silt to mist our masks

Clynton points deep into a dense tangle of nets

weighed down by bottles

I panic-gasp

as if it's me caught within

I peer in closer to find

the huge bulk of the humpback whale is trapped

inside

Is she alive?

Do I imagine her sonar moan

energy-sapped

choked by all our human filth

tears wash my eyes

remembering the story of myself

how I was found

wrapped in rubbish too

but still survived

That dream

coming here

somewhere deep inside I wonder

was this always meant

that it should be me

Immy

led here

to help set her free?

Clynton's already cutting through the net

pulse-pounds at my temples

chronometer inside my chest

thudding deafeningly loud

Carving a wide circle through the water with his hands, Clynton signs to me.

I think he's saying,

don't panic

Immy

witness

this day

you and I

are in touching distance of

a wonder of our world.

I'm not dreaming.

Everyone should know what it feels like to dive on the waking shore.

My mind is as clear as the waters of the Blue Planet should always be. The whale is as huge to me as I am to the tiny silver-backs that dart by as Clynton attempts to cut through the tangle of nets. The whale that's lost its way sits on the river bed and waits and waits, great eyelid closed at first, wrinkle-scored … strangely like the eye of an elephant.

I am a nothingness, a speck of dust, against her mass.

I hang in the water column and know I have to place my hand against her side, touch her, so she can feel me here, willing her to survive.

As I do

her huge eye

begins to open

In it

I see my world

and her world

mirrored

Her eye speaks into mine

How can you let me flounder?

Why don't you humans care?

And I know now, in my life, what I have to do.

The net gives as Clynton finally cuts his way through and raises his fist in triumph.

We summon all our strength to lift the net together.

Once, twice ... it's too heavy to shift. Thousands of plastic bottles weigh it down, locking the whale inside, making a noose for her, blocking her way out.

I start to throw the bottles away. It's heavy, slow work but Clynton nods, *the only thing to do* and joins me. We need more help. *Where is the Captain?*

I catch sight of an anchor on the river bed and *there he is* untangling an enormous knot. Looking up at me, he raises his arms in triumph and a rope floats free. With it the river sands send up a golden-silt-storm – or are those ... can they be?

The sparkling eyes of a million
seahorses lending us their power?

With one last blast of energy we lift
the net once more.

Slowly, slowly the whale begins to shift.

And the river bed tilts as she rises.

My chest aches, my heart aches, as trapped tears
    wash my cheek and I imagine them released,
    flowing into the waters of change and I
    know I will never be the driftwood-
    doubting Immy that I was before.

Clynton's at my side

reminding me to de-compress

when it's time

to make the slow rise

Chord surges rumble

The call of the River Whale is in me

Immy

I don't know where my will begins or the whale's will ends

but as I watch her brightening eye

all of me wishes her to survive

Let her thrive

Let her thrive

Let her thrive

Clynton holds me back and gestures for us to swim away and rise too, out of the enormous wake-wave the whale makes.

Her life force slowly builds and propels us to the surface too

just in time to see the sparkling diamond fountain of her

air-swallow

as she breaches

   the water

 and

     bathes in life.

I turn to *The Barnacle* boat, rocked and washed
by her waves, searching for Cosmo, still calling
my name.

I feel like I am born again

named again

looked for

cared for

squinting into light

dazed

There are cameras flashing from the bank. Clynton's hauling me along with him towards the River Cleaners. With a sigh of relief I spot the Captain climbing on to the platform. Then we follow. There's clapping but it feels far away. Limbs are heavy as stone. Oxygen cylinder is removed. Feeling lighter now Cosmo's near.

'How could you think to dive without anyone by your side? You know the rules!' But Clynton's look of pride, the triumph in his eyes doesn't match his ticking-off as he high-fives me.

'Where's the Captain?' I cast around *The Barnacle*.

'What Captain?' Clynton asks, the smile fading from his face. 'You're exhausted … disorientated.'

Sonar sound seeps from me.

Ears adjust. A camera flashes in my eye.

Cosmo shields me from the glare and wraps me in his arms.

I close my eyes and breathe in seahorse magic.

We get a lift in someone's van. As we rattle along, tandem clanking in the back, I ask what will happen to the River Whale now and Clynton says, 'We'll just have to hope she can be encouraged to swim back out to sea.'

Cosmo checks his phone … it's already news. I flush with pride to see the whale rising to the surface. There's me and Clynton but no sign of the Captain. 'Maybe because we climbed down different steps into the river?' I say, resting my head on Cosmo's shoulder but when we drop him off by the canal he whispers to me gently, 'Your dream came true, Immy, except for the Captain and the Tendril Teacher!'

As Clynton opens the van door, Mum and Dad are running down the steps smothering me with hugs, their eyes clouded with emotion, voices rushing over me. 'You were on the news, Immy. We've been at our wits' end with worry. Well, you're home now. At least you didn't come to any harm.'

One week later…

Chronometer's ticking.

Rubey can't stop purring.

It's like she senses Usha's coming home.

'How are we going to tell her everything that's happened since she left?' I whisper in Rubey's velvety ear.

Usha already knows about the whale … seems like everyone does! A journalist was pestering me outside the lido yesterday. Asked me if I'd heard the news – that the whale has found its way back out to sea and asking – have I got a comment because, if she wasn't mistaken, I am the girl who saved the 'River Whale'.

Rubey's purr grows loud as an engine as I carry her out among the swaying grasses of our top deck garden … waiting and watching the road. My heart leaps at Usha wild-waving, calling up to me that she's home. As if I can't see!

I set Rubey down and, pushing the Globe Window open, hurry through to our bedroom, checking out the black and white photo of Pops Michael saluting from the deck of a ferry boat as if he's saying a last farewell.

Smiling into his glinting eyes, I decide to say it how it is.

'Pops Michael. The more I look the more I know it's true … the Captain of *The Barnacle* was you!'

Bold adventure.

Breathtaking writing.

Dive into more books by

SITA BRAHMACHARI

If you enjoyed THE RIVER WHALE,
don't miss…

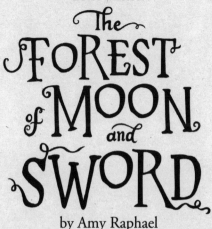

The FOREST of MOON and SWORD

by Amy Raphael

Twelve-year-old Art lives in a small village
in Scotland. Her mother has always made
potions that cure the sick, but now the
townspeople say she is a witch.

One cloudless night, Art's mother is accused
of Witchcraft, arrested, and taken from Scotland
to England. Art mounts her horse, taking a sword,
a tightrope, and a herbal recipe book
and begins a journey through wild forests to
find her mother before summer solstice.

On her journey, Art will discover the sacrifices
she'll need to make to be reunited with her mother.

But will she reach her, before it's too late?

Turn the page for the first chapter!

1

12 June 1647

I wake up in the dark.

I remember.

They are coming.

They will be here soon.

Word came this afternoon from the next village that the soldiers had crossed the border from England into Scotland, their weary horses hauling empty carts.

The wall is cold against my back. My body is stiff. I slowly stretch out my legs and the floorboard beneath me creaks.

'Art! Keep still,' whispers Mother.

We sit, my mother and I, in heavy silence.

I am suddenly glad of the dark because I can no longer see the desperation in her eyes.

'Hold my hand,' I say, so quietly that I don't expect her to respond. I place my hand on the dusty attic floor and she strokes it, her fingers as light and cold as the first snow, then wraps it in her hand and squeezes it tight.

I can barely hear the shallow breath of the women sitting on the other side of the attic. I have never met them before. They turned up at our house late this afternoon and told Mother they were scared their husbands might hand them over to the soldiers. Mother took them in and told them that as long they couldn't be seen or heard, they wouldn't be discovered. They are strangers, but I desperately want them to be safe.

I shut my eyes tight and try to imagine what I would be doing on an ordinary day. Perhaps Mother would be setting the fire against the last chill of spring while I read the Bible out loud to her. I would be hungry, as always. Oh, how hungry I am now, how thirsty. I try to stay still, but I need to use the chamber pot so badly.

I cannot leave the attic. Mother says hiding here is our best chance of evading capture. By the time the news of the soldiers came, it was too late to run. All we can do is wait. And hope against hope.

I huddle as close to Mother as possible, and she puts her mouth right up against my ear, so close that it tickles.

'Are you sure you know how to find the trapdoor in the dark?'

'Yes, Mother. And I am sure I will be able to

fit through it. We have practised enough times.' I immediately feel guilty for the edge in my voice, but I can't take it back.

We sit in silence before Mother speaks softly again. I know this story well. This is the story she tells to settle me when I have a fever, but this time I sense that I need to calm her too, so I squeeze her hand even tighter. 'When you were seven, I came home one afternoon to find you gone. I looked everywhere. I was beside myself. Eventually, as night was falling, I asked some townspeople to help search for you in the forest.' Her voice is unsteady. 'I thought you had been taken.'

It soothes me to remember that summer's morning, the mist burning off the fields and the sun already warm on my skin. I had seen a cloth sack on a neighbour's doorstep that was tied lightly at the top and that somehow seemed to be moving. Inside, I found four tiny kittens, three ginger and one pure black, all tiny and helpless, their mouths making silent mews as they blinked up at me. As I peered into the sack, the black kitten climbed above the others and pressed its face against mine. My heart soared. How I had longed for a black cat! Then my heart sank. At the bottom of the bag were three large stones, to weigh the sack down.

How could anybody plan to throw the sack in the river and drown these tiny, helpless kittens?

I removed the stones, threw them to the ground and ran, feeling the warmth of the kittens as I clutched the twitching sack to my chest.

I don't know how long I ran through the forest, but eventually I stopped by a small pond and set the sack down. The kittens looked up at me with their round, bright eyes, and a wave of pure love washed over me. I had saved them!

'When we finally found you by the pond, you were asleep and rigid with cold. The kittens you had tried so desperately to save had run away.' Mother sighs. 'All but one. Malkin was stretched out next to you, her black paws resting on your arm.'

Malkin. As black as night and as devoted to me as I was to her.

'I was furious,' says Mother, gently stroking my long, curly hair. 'I wanted to shake you to make you understand how much you'd scared me.'

Mother's face was drained of colour when she found Malkin and me. I looked up and saw her long red hair, as straight as an arrow, her face paler even than usual and flooded with concern, her green eyes brimming with tears. I had saved the kittens, but Mother had saved me. She always does.

She wrapped me in a woollen blanket and held me close, her heart beating furiously through her thin summer dress.

'I am so sorry about Malkin.' She squeezes my hand and continues. 'I know how much you loved her. You thought you'd never get over her death, but you are stronger than you think, Art Flynt.'

My beloved Malkin. Slaughtered less than a year ago by an unknown neighbour for being a so-called witch's cat. We mummified her body and laid her to rest inside the wall above the door, to ward off evil forces. I don't know why Mother doesn't think Malkin can help us now.

The attic is getting colder as the night deepens. I bring my legs up to my chest and rest my chin on my knees.

We sit in silence again.

A loud bang makes me jump. I stiffen.

'It's the wind playing with the stable door, Mother,' I whisper.

Mother's body is frozen with fear.

Another bang, this time louder and closer. The heavy wood of the front door being flung open.

Then – nothing.

The wind again. It must be the wind. Please let it be so.

I know Mother shut the front door carefully. I know it is not the wind.

'Search every room!' The voice booms through the house, as though the walls are made of paper and not thick, thick stone.

Mother's breath is warm in my ear. 'Aunt Elizabeth

will care for you. She is a strange sister, but I do believe that she will take you in with open arms. I love you, Art. Always. Carry me in your heart.' She puts her hand in her pocket and gives me something in the dark. 'Take this letter and read it only when it is safe to do so.'

I put it carefully in my pocket and open my mouth, but no words come. The footsteps on the wooden stairs are heavy and deliberate.

'Go, my child. Go now.'

'But, Mother …'

I don't move. I cannot say goodbye, not now, not like this. The footsteps are in the bedroom below. A man laughs as though this is some kind of game. I hear a chair being dragged along the floor, out of my bedroom and into the hallway. One of the soldiers pushes at the attic door. It always catches. Before, it made me cross. Now, it gives me time.

I jump to my feet. I locate the trapdoor above my head. Push the small square of wood aside. Pull myself up into the apex of the house. I have practised this so many times in the past few weeks, but always with Mother telling me what to do and praising my agility.

I can hear the attic door below being lifted up.

I push the trapdoor back in place and crouch on top of it.

'Traitors! Witches! *Scottish* witches! You will burn in hell.' The soldier's voice is ablaze with pure hatred.

My mouth is dry. I cannot swallow. My legs shake uncontrollably. I shut my eyes and count slowly, as Mother told me to.

100. 99. 98. 97. 96. 95.

One of the women emits a high-pitched wail as she is lowered through the attic door.

'Silence, woman! Silence, all of you!'

The soldier's tone is so sharp that the woman falls silent. All I can hear is muffled voices as the soldiers direct Mother and the women out of the attic and down the stairs.

50. 49. 48.

The front door slams.

Now I am alone.

10. 9. 8.

My legs are shaking hard. I can no longer feel my feet.

3. 2. 1.

I breathe in and out slowly before standing up. The space is narrow but tall, with a small window on one side. I look out across the fields, biting my nails. The moon is bright and the puddles on the track leading away from the farm are finally starting to dry up after weeks of rain. If I balance on the old milking stool, I can just about see the four soldiers and their horses and carts. The horses stand patiently, occasionally flicking their tails, unaware of what is happening around them.

I long to put my arms around my own horse's neck, but Lady will have to wait.

One of the soldiers lines up the women. I can see the first three women, but the remaining three, including Mother, are just out of sight.

I strain to hear. 'Do what I say and no one will be hurt,' says the chief soldier. He stands with his legs apart, one hand thrust deep in his pocket and the other pulling at his huge beard as though it is some kind of prize. He is as vain as Uncle Samuel, who used to admire himself in the polished stone every Sunday morning before church.

The women stare at the ground.

The chief soldier reaches into the cart closest to him and throws a coil of coarse rope at another soldier. 'Hastings, tie them up.'

'Yes, sir.'

Whoever Hastings is takes a knife from his belt and starts cutting the rope.

'Five of you will be executed at dawn,' says the chief soldier. 'There will be a short trial first. We know you are all guilty of being witches, of course, so think of the trial as a mere formality. One of you will be taken straight to England.'

Who? Who will be saved? The thought that it might not be Mother chills my blood.

Hastings stands behind the woman at the start of

the line and wrenches her hands behind her back. He wraps the rope around her wrists three times, pulling it until she flinches. He walks methodically along the line tying up each of the women's wrists.

'Throw them in the cart,' says the chief soldier.

Hastings pushes one woman into the cart as though she is an animal. He pushes another. A third.

Mother must be standing with the other two women, but I cannot see her.

I stand on tiptoes on the stool. As it sways, I grab hold of the window ledge. The stool falls and I tumble to the floor. Fool! *What if they heard me?*

As I jump to my feet and step back on to the stool, the chief soldier below laughs so hard that I think he must have lost his reason. But at least he doesn't look up. He doesn't know I'm here.

Clouds obscure the moon. I wipe away some of the dirt on the window with my sleeve, though still I see only darkness. I allow myself a moment to remember all those times my best friend Cecily and I used to hang out of the attic window and blow at the clouds until they drifted away from the sun, laughing so hard when the sun reappeared that our stomachs hurt.

'Please,' I whisper, squeezing my eyes shut. 'Please let me see Mother one last time.'

When I open my eyes, the clouds have vanished and the moon is bright.

Malkin is helping me!

The soldiers are guiding the horses and carts down the dirt track. The wheels bump in and out of puddles. One of the soldiers leans to the side and spits into the earth. Leaving a marker behind and taking Mother away. Taking away everything I have.

Five women huddle together in the first cart, their faces hidden. I stare and stare at the solitary woman in the second cart, at the woman who is to be taken to England, to a fate unknown.

As the second cart turns a bend, I see the woman glance up at the attic window.

I see Mother.

On your bookmarks, get set, read!

Well hello there! We are

Overjoyed that you have joined our celebration of

Reading books and sharing stories, because we

Love bringing books to you.

Did you know, we are a charity dedicated to celebrating the

Brilliance of reading for pleasure for everyone, everywhere?

Our mission is to help you discover brand new stories and

Open your mind to exciting worlds and characters, from

Kings and queens to wizards and pirates to animals and adventurers and so many more. We couldn't

Do it without all the amazing authors and illustrators, booksellers and bookshops, publishers, schools and libraries out there –

And most importantly, we couldn't do it all without . . .

You!

Changing lives through a love of books and shared reading.

World Book Day is a registered charity funded by publishers and booksellers in the UK & Ireland.

Share a story

From breakfast to bedtime, there's always time to discover and share stories together. You can . . .

1 Take a trip to your local bookshop

Brimming with brilliant books and helpful booksellers to share awesome reading recommendations, you can also enjoy booky events with your favourite authors and illustrators.

Find your local bookshop:
booksellers.org.uk/bookshopsearch

2 Join your local library

That wonderful place where the hugest selection of books you could ever want to read awaits – and you can borrow them for FREE! Plus expert advice and fantastic free family reading events.

Find your local library:
gov.uk/local-library-services/

3 Check out the World Book Day website

Looking for reading tips, advice and inspiration? There is so much to discover at **worldbookday.com**, packed with fun activities, audiobooks, videos, competitions and all the latest book news galore.